Deputy Paws
and the Puppy Mill Cause

by Peggy Race

Illustrations by Mike Motz

For Deputy, my muse

May the echo of your words,
inspire others to act on behalf of those,
whose voices sit silenced
behind a wall of greed.

Acknowledgments

Throughout the process of bringing this book to life, many individuals have given of their time to make my dream a reality. Working with a group of such talented individuals is a gift, in and of itself.

This book would not have been possible without the support and encouragement of AllWriters' Workplace and Workshop, writing coach, Carrie Newberry, whose keen eye and dog loving touch helped refine and improve the story line.

Thank you, Susan Nies, for tapping the table to each beat in order to test for correct meter. It was music to my ears.

My deepest thanks to the National Mill Dog Rescue for not only rescuing Deputy and allowing me to adopt him but for the life-saving work they do to bring dogs to freedom.

I would like to express my gratitude to Mindi Callison, founder of Bailing Out Benji. I am honored to be a volunteer with this organization.

A special thanks to Mike Motz and his crew who captured not only the heart of the story, but brought to life Deputy's character in a fun and engaging manner. Watching my words come to life has been an amazing adventure.

I wish to recognize Tom Ganser for his photographic expertise which captured the heartfelt happiness of my canine family.

Many thanks to Life Coach Pat Jones for being my cheerleader and advocate on this journey.

I wish to thank my mom, Suzanne Rudolph, my sister, Paula Rudolph Brown, and the many people who listened, offered support, and gave of their time as I asked for feedback and bounced around my ideas.

Finally, I wish to thank Deputy for being the inspiration behind bringing my voice to life.

A portion of profits from this book will be donated to
animal rescues, shelters and organizations
who promote animal welfare.

Welcome, dear friends!
I'm Deputy Paws,
here to explore
the puppy mill cause.

I'm a proud rescue
who was born in a mill.
I'm sharing my story
for those living there still.

Puppy mill dogs
spend their lives in a cage,
all for the sake
of the mill breeder's wage.

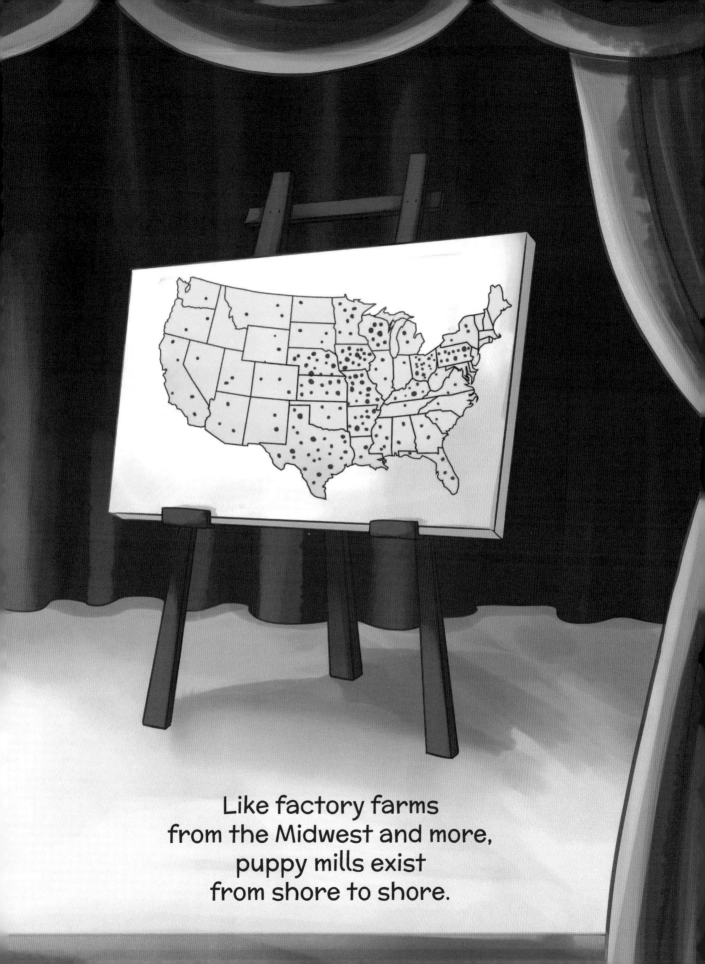

Like factory farms
from the Midwest and more,
puppy mills exist
from shore to shore.

From Cockers to Labs
and Designer Dogs, too,
they live in a world
that is hidden from view.

It's such a sad truth
I'm here to proclaim –
Wealth outweighs health.
The laws are too lame.

I'm raising awareness
through my actions and voice.
Adoption, my friends,
must be the right choice.

Follow my journey
and where it does lead.
I'll shine a bright light
on what dogs really need.

WATER

I'm Deputy Paws.
I remember it still –
the sick little puppies
who lived in the mill.

The costs are too high
for a pill or a shot,
so health is forgotten
more often than not.

I love my new home
and trips to the vet.
It's one of the ways
my needs are now met.

I remember the day
I was dealt a bad hand.
I lived on thin wire,
not grass or soft land.

Food and fresh water
were scarce every day.
There wasn't a place
to run or to play.

I now have a bed
and food in my bowl.
I love the backyard
where I romp and I roll.

Recipe: Puppy Mill Dog
Ingredients:
1 Mom
1 Dad
Place dogs into a cage.
Place cage in barn.
Add:
6 Puppies
Directions:
Sprinkle with food and water
Do not add heat
Do not supply toys
Do not provide vet care
Let all dogs sit in cage for 7-8 weeks
Remove puppies and send to pet store
Repeat every 6 months.

108

I felt all alone;
in a cage I did stir,
with filth on my coat
and mats in my fur.

From the heat of the day
to the cold of the night,
I lived in conditions
that just were not right.

My nails are now trim
and my coat, it does shine.
I'm feeling the love
in a home that is mine.

I was one of those dogs,
set aside like the trash.
The breeder he thought,
I would bring him no cash.

National Mill Dog
was the rescue who came.
They brought me to freedom
and gave me a name.

I lived at their shelter.
There was love all around.
They gave me great care,
'til my new home was found.

I stand here today,
I'm happy to share.
My life it was changed
by people who care.

Adoption and rescue
for me are the key,
that opened my cage
and helped set me free.

I'm one of those puppies
who was born in a mill.
There are many more like me
that need your help still.

I'll give you some tools
to put to good use,
to find your own voice
and help end this abuse.

Learn all that you can
before you walk through the door.
It's the mill dogs who suffer
when you buy from the store.

Don't spend your money
on a pup at the store.
Squeeze out their profits.
They'll close the front door.

Break the connection
from breeder to store.
Go to your shelter!
Adopt and adore!

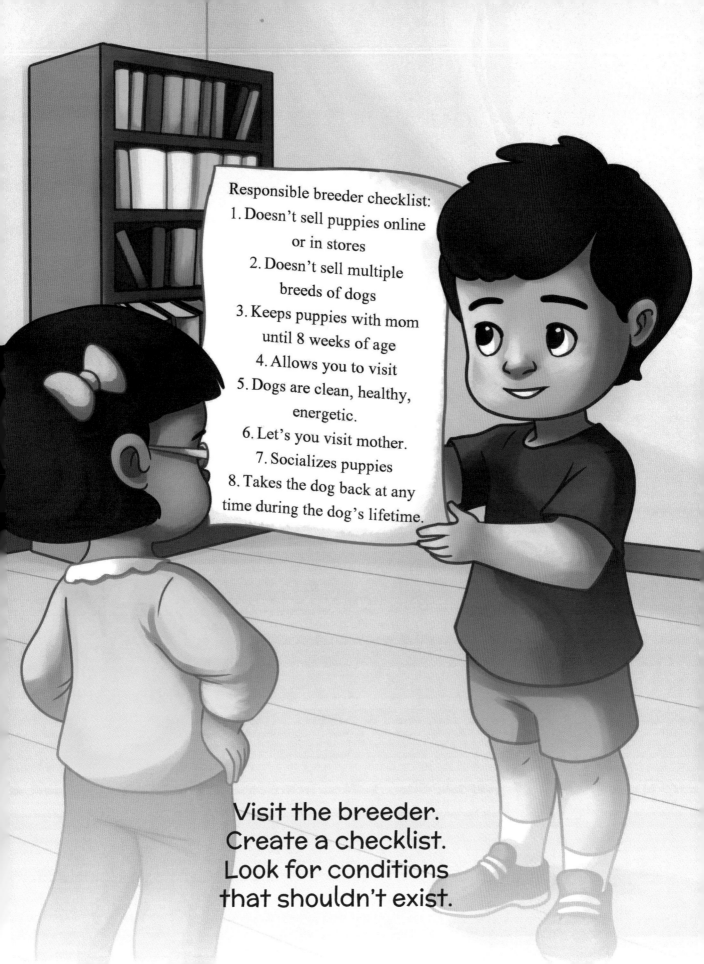

Wave a red flag
as a big warning sign
when pups are for sale
in ads or online.

Don't get fooled by the ads
fueled by greed and by wealth.
Remember the mill dogs
who live in poor health.

Raise up your voices
and take a strong stand.
Be part of the change
across our great land.

Contact your Senator,
and Congressman, too.
Reform of the laws
is long overdue.

Write to the papers,
or post notes online.
For animal welfare,
a light we must shine.

Protest the pet stores.
Their actions must shift.
Promoting adoption
would be a facelift.

I know from my past
the cycle, it stopped.
Don't buy from the pet store.
Please rescue and adopt!

I dream of the day
all dogs are set free,
to live in a home
like you and like me.

Visit your shelter
or local rescue.
For change to take place,
it all starts with you.

I ask of you, please,
be part of a trend.
Give your support
to this cause I defend.

Adoption saves lives.
On you they depend.
Adopt your next dog
and make a new friend!

A puppy mill is a dog breeding business in which dogs are bred for profit. Similar to a factory farm style of operation, the business prioritizes monetary gain over the health and welfare of the dogs. In order to maximize profits, quality food, water, veterinary care, and housing are kept to a minimum. The dogs receive little to no human contact or socialization.

Breeding dogs will live their lives in a cage until their bodies can no longer reproduce. At that time, the dogs are either disposed of or in some cases, surrendered to a rescue organization.

Puppies born in puppy mills are often removed from their mother prior to 8 weeks of age. They are often sick due to the poor conditions in which they are born. Puppy mill dogs are sold in pet stores and online.

For more information

milldogrescue.org   bailingoutbenji.com   bestfriends.org

aspca.org   humanesociety.org

Documentary: *Dog By Dog*   ASIN: B01LTI0KTC

Recommended reading:

The Doggie in the Window by Rory Kress

ISBN 978-1-49265182-6

Bark Until Heard by Becky Monroe

ISBN 978-1-50784124-2

About the Author

Peggy Race is a Wisconsin-based children's book author, literary memoir writer, and avid dog lover with a vision to create a better world for our canine companions.

  To date, she has completed various dog handling workshops, was an intern in Dog Town at Best Friends Animal Society, and has spent her time volunteering for numerous other esteemed organizations. Peggy has dabbled in dog sports, competing in agility and taking nosework classes. Currently, Peggy serves as a volunteer for Bailing Out Benji, an organization which raises awareness of and educates about puppy mills and their connection to pet stores.

  Peggy shares her home with three fun-loving dogs: Desiree, a rescue from Hurricane Katrina; Faith, a ball herding border collie; and Deputy, a cocker spaniel mix, rescued from a puppy mill, and the inspiration behind *Deputy Paws and the Puppy Mill Cause.*

Photo by Tom Ganser (Whitewater, WI)

Made in the USA
Columbia, SC
01 September 2018